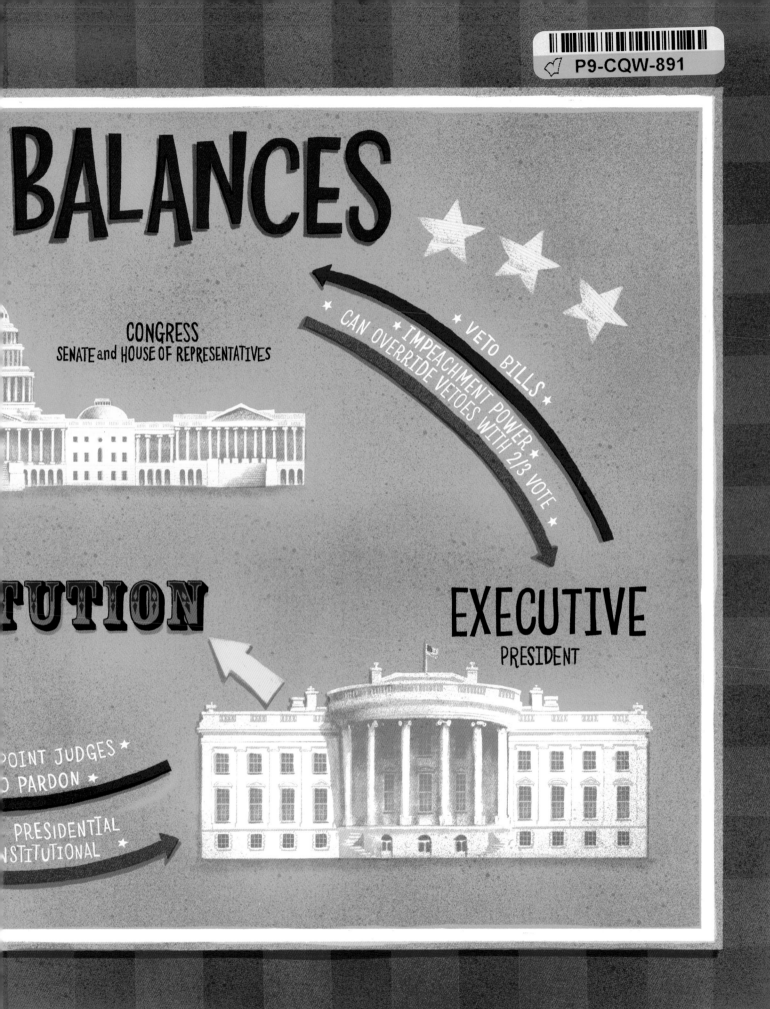

# BALANCES

CONGRESS
SENATE and HOUSE OF REPRESENTATIVES

★ VETO BILLS ★
★ IMPEACHMENT POWER ★
CAN OVERRIDE VETOES WITH 2/3 VOTE

TUTION

EXECUTIVE
PRESIDENT

POINT JUDGES ★
PARDON ★

PRESIDENTIAL
STITUTIONAL

For Havana, a true leader—K.D.
To Nova and Roen, who are out to change the world—L.P.

First Edition, September 2019
10 9 8 7 6 5 4 3 2 1
FAC-029191-19200
Printed in Malaysia

The quotation on page 19 is reprinted by arrangement with The Heirs to the Estate of Martin Luther King, Jr.,
c/o Writers House as agent for the proprietor New York, NY.
Quotation copyright © 1959 Dr. Martin Luther King, Jr. © renewed 1987 Coretta Scott King

This book is set in Caslon Antique/Fontspring and Chevalier Pro/Linotype
Designed by Joann Hill

Library of Congress Cataloging-in-Publication Data
Names: DiPucchio, Kelly, author. • Pham, LeUyen, illustrator.
Title: Grace goes to Washington / by Kelly DiPucchio ; pictures by LeUyen Pham.
Description: First edition. • Los Angeles : Disney Hyperion, 2019. •
Summary: On a school field trip to Washington, D.C., student council member Grace and
her classmates learn about the three branches of the federal government, how school
government operates, the qualities of effective leadership, and how to be a good citizen.
Identifiers: LCCN 2018053227 • ISBN 9781368024334 (hardcover) • ISBN 1368024335 (hardcover)
Subjects: • CYAC: United States—Politics and government—Fiction. • Political participation—Fiction. •
School field trips—Fiction. • African Americans—Fiction. • Washington (D.C.)—Fiction.
Classification: LCC PZ7.D6219 Gs 2019 • DDC [E]—dc23
LC record available at https://lccn.loc.gov/2018053227

Reinforced binding
Visit www.DisneyBooks.com

# GRACE ★ GOES TO ★ WASHINGTON

by

Kelly
DiPucchio

pictures by

LeUyen
Pham

𝒟ISNEY • HYPERION
LOS ANGELES   NEW YORK

One Friday afternoon in April, Mrs. Barrington shared a large diagram of the three branches of the US government. But Grace Campbell could not stop daydreaming about the upcoming field trip to Washington, DC.

"Grace, do you know who's in charge here?" Mrs. Barrington asked.

"Who's in charge here?" Grace repeated. "Principal Pérez?" A few of her classmates giggled.

"Well," said Mrs. Barrington, "I suppose you could say Principal Pérez is like the executive branch here at Wilson Elementary, because she's the head of our school, but right now we're talking about the US government."

"Sorry," Grace answered. "The president. He, *or she*, leads the executive branch."

"That's correct!" Mrs. Barrington smiled. "The president."

The last bell of the day rang. "We'll discuss this more next week," she announced. "Student council members Grace and Sam, don't forget you have a meeting after school!"

At the meeting, classroom representatives
were discussing their ideas on how to spend the
money raised from their holiday bake sale.

Thomas and his committee petitioned for new sports equipment.

Grace and her committee thought new books for the library was the way to go.

Principal Pérez even offered her own suggestion.

Mr. Marshall, the media-center teacher, listened
carefully to all of their arguments and took notes.

"They're all good ideas," Grace later admitted to Sam.
"There's no way we'll agree before the vote next week."

"You know what I was thinking during the meeting?" Sam asked.

"No, what?"

LEGISLATIVE BRANCH

EXECUTIVE BRANCH

"If Principal Pérez is like the executive branch, I think the student council is kind of like the legislative branch, because we're the elected leaders from each class and we help make decisions for the school."

Grace considered Sam's comparison. "Yeah, who knew so many people had a say in how to spend cookie money?" she grumbled.

The following day, Grace could hardly contain her excitement.
**IT WAS FINALLY FIELD-TRIP DAY!**

SCHOOL BUS

As the bus drove down Pennsylvania Avenue, cherry
blossoms dotted the streets like pink pom-poms.

Grace and her classmates
visited the Lincoln Memorial . . .

. . . the US Capitol, where the
legislative branch meets . . .

. . . and the Supreme Court Building.

"That's where you'll find the judicial branch and Supreme Court judges," Sam pointed out. "They decide if our rules and laws are fair."

"Kind of like Mr. Marshall does at our student council meetings!" Grace added.

During a tour of the White House, home of the executive branch, Grace's dream of becoming president felt more real.

Their final stop of the day was the Martin Luther King, Jr. Memorial.

Grace studied the words engraved on the
monument and thought about their meaning.

MAKE A CAREER OF HUMANITY. COMMIT YOURSELF TO THE NOBLE
STRUGGLE FOR EQUAL RIGHTS. YOU WILL MAKE A GREATER
PERSON OF YOURSELF, A GREATER NATION OF YOUR
COUNTRY AND A FINER WORLD TO LIVE IN.

At recess the next day, arguments about what to purchase for the school grew more heated.

"Look at this crummy basketball!" Clara complained. "It's practically worthless."

"At least you have a ball!" Fletcher groaned. "There are two new books in the Ninja Wizard series, but our library doesn't have either one."

Hannah lobbied the loudest for new instruments. "Well, I for one am sick and tired of playing the recorder in music class! Principal Pérez is right!"

Grace glanced at Thomas, who was
unusually quiet. She looked past
him to see who he was staring at.

Grace didn't recognize the
boy sitting all alone.

*He must be new*, she thought.
He looked kind of sad.

Just then the bell rang, and students scattered.

"Wait!" Grace called out to the boy.
"You forgot something!"

Grace handed him his sketchbook.
"I like your drawing," she said.

"Thanks," said the
boy with a smile.

Grace caught up to Thomas in the hallway.
"I have an idea," she said.

A few days later, the student council's last
meeting of the year was being called to order.

The blackboard reads:

Bake Sale Profits
VOTE TODAY!!!

"Excuse me," Grace interrupted. "Before we vote,
Thomas and I would like to introduce you to someone.

This is Aman. He's new to our school. We'd like all of you to consider one more option for how to spend the bake-sale money."

Together, they rolled out a big poster.

"We're calling it the Friendship Mall!" Thomas said proudly. "Aman helped us design it."

"It's a place where you can go at recess to let other students know when you need a friend," Aman explained.

Next, Thomas spoke about their field trip to Washington, DC, and Grace read a quote from Martin Luther King, Jr.

"A finer, kinder world starts with us and the choices we make,"

she concluded.
"Thank you for listening."

Everyone clapped. Principal Pérez wiped away a few tears.
Mr. Marshall pounded his gavel. "It's time to vote!"

After the ballots were collected from each classroom representative and the votes were tallied, student council president Grace Campbell peeked at the results and grinned.
"It's a unanimous decision," she announced excitedly.

All members are in favor of . . .

... THE FRIENDSHIP MALL!

The room filled with happy cheers. Principal
Pérez took a seat and then, much like the
president signs a bill into law, she approved the
election results, making the decision official.

"Today you put your own wants and needs aside
in order to serve others," she said, beaming.
"That is true leadership!"

This time, everyone agreed.

## Author's Note

You may have heard about the three branches of government, but what exactly are they and what do they do? First of all, the branches have nothing to do with trees. They were created by our nation's Founding Fathers when they wrote the US Constitution in 1787. Each unique branch was designed with its own set of responsibilities, but they all work together to help govern our country.

Let's take a closer look at what the three branches are and some of the jobs they do.

**The Executive Branch:** The president of the United States leads this branch. The president has the power to recommend new laws, reject laws, and sign bills into laws. He or she is also in charge of our armed forces, which is why we sometimes refer to the president as the Commander-in-Chief.

**The Legislative Branch:** This branch of government is comprised of Congress. Congress is made up of two groups—the House of Representatives and the Senate. These elected officials are our states' representatives and senators. Their job is to pass bills and make laws for our country. The Legislative Branch also has the power to reject a president's ruling, and they can vote to remove the president from office.

The Judicial Branch: This third branch is made up of the highest court in the country—the Supreme Court. There are nine Supreme Court judges, called *justices*. They do not make laws. They make decisions about laws to determine if they are fair based on the US Constitution. Whereas the Executive Branch and the Legislative Branch are elected by the people, the Judicial Branch is chosen by the president and approved by the Senate.

You might be wondering why we need three separate branches of government instead of one big branch. The Constitution created a system of *checks and balances* to prevent one branch from having too much power. We call this the *separation of powers*. This is a very important feature in the way our democratic government operates, because it keeps the system fair and just and it protects the rights of the people.

While many of you reading this are too young to vote for the leaders who represent our country and make our laws, you are never too young to get involved. You can become a leader in your school or in your community, like Grace. Your voice matters! You matter! And you can make a difference, too.

–K.D.

# How can you become an involved citizen and make a difference?

☆ Start a civics club in your school for students interested in developing their leadership skills through community involvement and civic responsibility.

☆ Take a guided tour of your state capitol building or city hall to learn more about the legislative process, as well as the architecture and history of the building.

☆ Learn about the United States Constitution and the Bill of Rights. Write your own constitution for your family or classroom.

☆ Go with a parent or family member to the polls on Election Day.

☆ Write a letter to the president, your state's governor, or another elected official telling him or her about your concerns or your ideas for the future.

☆ Attend a political event or rally with family or friends.

☆ Research political candidates and/or proposals and make your own campaign posters.

☆ Inspire a community of inclusion and cultural understanding by learning more about the diverse traditions, food, clothing, language, and celebrations of people living in your neighborhood.

☆ Attend a local city council meeting.

☆ Create your own newspaper highlighting notable events, people, and programs in your community or in the country.

☆ Donate food, clothing, books, or your time to local organizations that are helping people in need in your community.

☆ Suggest holding a mock election in your classroom.

☆ Visit your local and state historical museums.

☆ Identify one thing you feel could make your community a better place to live. Brainstorm ways you can actively make a difference in this area.

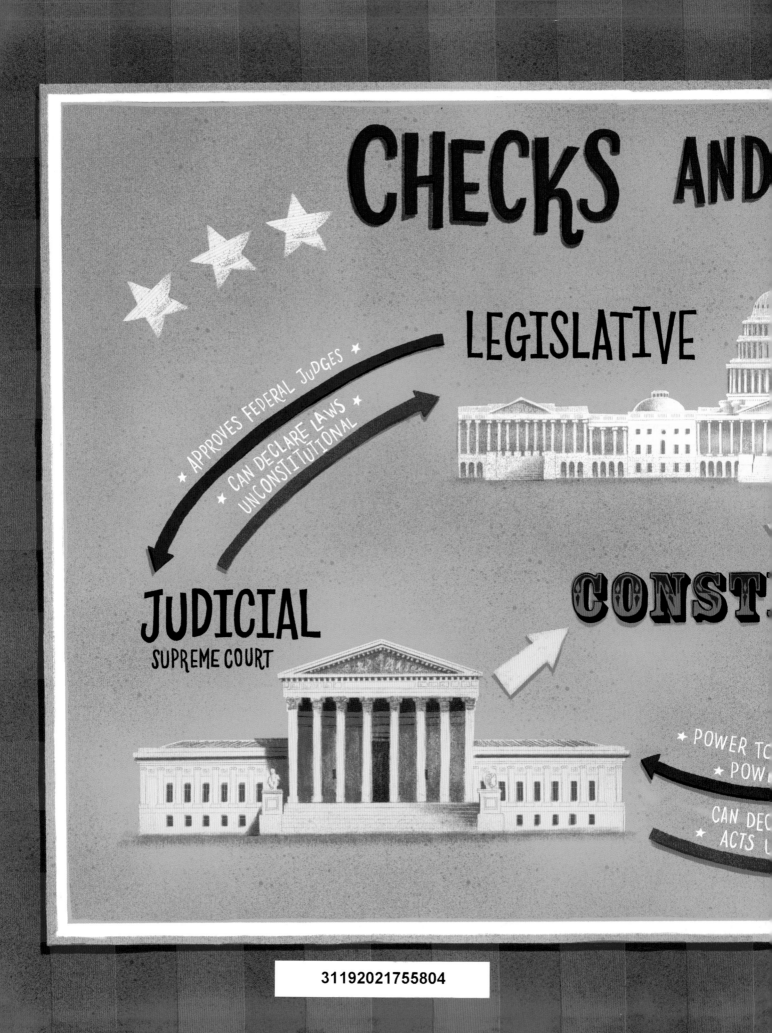